PAC
10/06

THREE BILLY GOATS GRUFF

For Patricia Rounds, the mother of my granddaughters, with much love

Library of Congress Cataloging-in-Publication Data
Rounds, Glen, 1906–
Three billy goats Gruff / retold and illustrated
by Glen Rounds. — 1st. ed.
p.   cm.
Summary: Retells the folktale about three billy goats
who trick a troll that lives under a bridge.
ISBN 0-8234-1015-3
[1. Fairy tales. 2. Folklore—Norway.]   I. Asbjørnsen,
Peter Christen, 1812–1885. Tre bukkene Bruse. II. Title.
III. Title: 3 billy goats Gruff.
PZ8.R775Th   1993   92-23951   CIP   AC
398.24'5297358'09481—dc20
[E]

ISBN 0-8234-1136-2 (pbk.)

THREE BILLY GOATS GRUFF

retold and illustrated by
Glen Rounds

Holiday House/New York

Once on a time, there were three billy goats.

One was very small, one was middle-sized, and one was very large.

They were all named GRUFF, so people simply called them

THE THREE BILLY GOATS GRUFF.

On a certain morning, the Three Billy Goats Gruff were on their way to a distant hillside where the grass was especially tall and green and tender.

But to get to the hillside, they had to cross a bridge over a DEEP, SWIFT RIVER.

AND UNDER THAT BRIDGE LIVED A
GREAT, BIG, UGLY TROLL!

The smallest Billy Goat Gruff had just started
across the bridge, trip-trap, trip-trap, trip-trap,
when the troll roared from below,

"WHO'S THAT TRIPPING ACROSS MY BRIDGE?"

"It's only me, the smallest Billy Goat Gruff," the little billy goat answered in his tiny voice. "I'm going over to yonder hillside where the grass is so tall and green and tender."

"NO, YOU'RE NOT," roared the troll, "BECAUSE I'M GOING TO EAT YOU UP!"

"Oh, no!" cried the billy goat, "please don't eat me up! I'm much too small to make a meal for you! Wait for the second Billy Goat Gruff—he's MUCH bigger than I am!"

"Well, maybe you're right," growled the troll, "so be off with you!"

And he went back down under the bridge while the little billy goat ran to the green hillside beyond.

Then the second Billy Goat Gruff started
across the bridge,

trip-trap, trip-trap, trip-trap,
and again the troll roared,

"WHO'S TRIPPING ACROSS MY BRIDGE?"

"It's me, the second Billy Goat Gruff. But please don't eat me. The biggest Billy Goat Gruff is right behind me, and he is MUCH bigger!"

"Well," growled the troll, "get on with you. I'll wait for the big one!"

So the second billy goat ran safely across the bridge and to the green hillside beyond.

Then the BIGGEST billy goat stamped onto the bridge,

trip-trap, trip-trap, trip-trap!

And again the troll roared in his loudest voice,

"WHO'S THAT TRAMPING OVER MY BRIDGE?"

"It's me, the BIGGEST BILLY GOAT GRUFF!" shouted the billy goat in a voice almost as loud as the troll's.

"WHOEVER YOU ARE, I'M
GOING TO EAT YOU UP
RIGHT NOW!" roared the troll.

AND HE CLIMBED ONTO
THE TOP OF THE BRIDGE.

"Well, come on then!" cried the big billy goat. "I've got sharp horns to butt you with! And hard hooves to trample you with!"

THAT'S WHAT THE BIG BILLY GOAT SAID.

THEN THE BIG BILLY GOAT
RAN AT THE TROLL

AND THE TROLL RAN AT
THE BILLY GOAT!

The big billy goat butted the ugly troll with his hard horns and trampled him with his sharp hooves.

Then he butted him again and knocked him off the bridge and into the DEEP, SWIFT RIVER BELOW.

The big billy goat stomped on across the bridge and onto the hillside where the grass was so tall and green and tender.

The great ugly troll was never seen again, and if the three Billy Goats Gruff haven't gone away, they are still on that hillside, getting fatter every day.

And now, as Grandmother used to say,

"Snip! Snap! Snout!
This tale's told out!"